Nettie Cyberland

Book 1 of
Nettie's Internet
Safety Books

Wendy Goucher

illustrated by Jim Barker

University of Buckingham Press, 51 Gower Street, London, WC1E 6HJ
info@unibuckinghampress.com | www.unibuckinghampress.com

Text and Illustrations © Wendy Goucher, 2020
Illustrations by Jim Barker, 2020

Print: 9781800319844
Ebook: 9781800319851

Set in Aniara. Printing managed by Jellyfish Solutions Ltd
Cover design and layout by Rachel Lawston, lawstondesign.com

INTRODUCTION

I wrote this book with two dreams in mind.

Firstly, I wanted to help small children who are using computers, tablets and phones learn that they have to take care, just like when they cross the road. We don't wait for our children to need to cross the road by themselves before we teach them about road safety; we start talking about crossing when the green man lights up while they are still in a buggy. The sooner children learn how to cross safely, the safer they will be, even when they learn harder road safety such as crossing without signals. We can introduce "cyber safety" in a similar fashion - simple ideas for a child to learn as they use the Internet for different things, and in different ways.

Secondly, I want you - the adults who are reading this story to children - to be able to talk to the children about safety in Cyberland, or the Internet. Nettie's adventures are a way of opening a dialogue with children about behaving in a safe manner. As I developed this book, many adults told me that they don't know where to start talking about computer safety with children; it makes them afraid and powerless, even "useless", because they don't have all the answers. But if you start the conversation while the child is young, that trust will encourage them to tell you about what they see, what other children tell them, and what they like or dislike about the Internet. Your knowledge can grow with theirs.

At the end of this book I have put website addresses for trusted resources that can help you understand the subject more, and find clear, detailed answers to questions this book doesn't cover. You may find some things that you can share with the child in your care, expanding your discussion of safety beyond Nettie's stories.

Most of all, this story is not designed to make children anxious about the Internet (or, in this story, Cyberland). It is here to help them learn how to behave sensibly. At the end of the story Nettie isn't hurt, or missing in a dark forest: she is home safe in bed. That is the most important message of all. At the end of the day, children want places of trust and safety they can retreat to, and that's where you come in.

Today is a wet and rainy day.

Grandad has taken the dog Charlie for a walk, but Nettie forgot her wellingtons, so she can't go with them.

Nettie likes to make a house out of Grandma's tablecloth to play in with her toys.

She loves to draw and colour pictures in her book.

She loves to sing to her toys. They think she is very good.

After a while Nettie is getting bored of singing and drawing.

"The rain must be gone by now," she thinks.

So, she looks out of the window.

It hasn't stopped; it is as wet as ever.

She remembers Grandad's tablet, which she uses to play
music on. Nettie isn't allowed to use it without asking,
but she is bored and she wouldn't break it.

Nettie wants to go on the Internet to play games.
So when Grandma isn't looking she takes
the tablet into her little house.

Suddenly Grandma's face appears around the
side of the tent. She looks very cross.

"Nettie, you know you aren't allowed to play with
the tablet unless Grandad or I say it's OK."

So, Grandma takes the tablet and puts
it in Grandad's workshop.

Nettie is furious.

Grandma tries to explain that the tablet is Grandad's,
and Nettie needs to ask before she takes things.

But Nettie isn't really listening.

A little while later Grandma is watching her favourite TV
show and Nettie sneaks into Grandad's workshop.

Grandad is an inventor. Nettie thinks his workshop is full of interesting things, but Grandma says some of it is "positively unsafe". Nettie is not allowed to go in on her own, but today she is so cross she doesn't care. When she opens the door, the room is dark, but she can still see dials and fans and shiny objects all over the room.

Then Nettie sees the tablet between a ball and a toy shaped like an egg.

It is so high up that she has to climb onto a box to reach it. Even then Nettie has to reach out, standing on the very tips of her toes.

Nettie tipples and wobbles, and then she falls.

Nettie can't fly, but she doesn't hit the ground either.
Instead, she's falling right into Grandad's tablet.

Then "BUMP" – Nettie lands on soft, bouncy grass.
In a flash, the tablet appears beside her.

Nettie looks around and finds the egg toy that had been
in Grandad's workshop. It must've fallen in with her.

The egg toy quickly gets big, with long floppy arms and bendy legs.
It also has the biggest, happiest smile Nettie has ever seen on an egg.

"Hello, I'm Webby," says the egg.

"Where are we, Webby?" Nettie asks.

"Grown-ups call this 'The Internet', we call it 'Cyberland.'"

"Oh, I love the Internet," says Nettie. "There are games and cute pictures of bunnies and cats and dogs."

"Well," said Webby, "Cyberland is a really big place – that's why I have long legs and a comfy seat for you in my dome."

So Nettie climbs in. "Put the little tablet on the shelf in front of you," says Webby. You can talk to me through it and tell me what to do."

"Let's go see the bunnies," Nettie says.

So that's what they did.

Webby finds some bunnies in no time at all. They jump on his dome and it makes Nettie laugh.

They also sniff at his feet, and that makes Webby chuckle.

Time to Talk

On the next page the story pauses to give you the chance to talk to your child about using computers and phones and tablets.

There are some questions to help, but it is best if you are able to listen to the answers the child gives, and maybe ask your own questions as well.

There is more help at the end of the story.

At this point there are no right or wrong answers. It is to help the child to talk about what they understand. They will learn later one good reason for not being allowed to use the Internet without supervision, but it is better if they work this out for themselves, rather than being told.

Let's talk

Nettie likes to look at bunnies. What do you like
to do on the tablet, computer or phone?

I like to see... I like to play...

Nettie isn't allowed to play with the tablet unless
a grown-up says say it's OK. Why do you think that is?

Maybe because...

What are your favourite Internet sites?

I like the game Dad found for me ...it's fun!

They all play together for ages
and get very tired, so they
take a nap in the warm sun.

Nettie notices a forest that looks
very interesting. There is a big sign
that says "Keep out", but Nettie thinks
that this is silly: it's just a forest.

She is sure someone is just trying to stop her having
fun – like Grandma did with the tablet.

So she wakes Webby up to take her into the forest.
Webby is not happy.

"But Nettie, the sign says 'Keep Out.'"

"That's a silly sign, Webby, and you have to do
what I say. Let's go," Nettie insists.

Nervously Webby tiptoes towards the forest.

The forest is dark.

The trees are not green or nice.

There are no flowers or bunnies or any cute animals, no matter how hard Nettie looks. This isn't what Nettie imagined at all. What are they going to do?

Then something lands on Webby's dome.

All around them are creepy, hungry creatures.

They are green and slimy and ugly and make Webby scared.

"Oh dear," Nettie thinks, "I'm going to be in such trouble.
Grandma told me not to go on the Internet on my own."

Then one of the creatures plants a big, sloppy
monstery kiss on Webby's dome.

Webby starts to sway and squeal. "Nettie, help, I can't see!
You must press the big red button: it will send us home to safety."

Nettie realises that she is more frightened of the
creatures than she is of Grandma being cross.

"Webby's in danger, I have to be brave. Even if I get in
trouble with Grandma I have to send us home."

So, Nettie presses the big red button.

With a "Whoosh" they are back. Nettie lands on the floor of Grandad's workshop. She is still holding little Webby.

Nettie catches her breath, she starts to cry. She hears Grandad come back in the house with Charlie and she runs upstairs.

Grandad hears the sound of Nettie's crying and he follows it all the way back to Nettie's room.

When he gently opens the door, Grandad and Charlie find Nettie on her bed crying. So he quietly calls Grandma and they all cuddle up close on the bed.

"What's wrong Nettie? Why are you so sad?" they ask.

Then she tells them the whole story.

Grandma goes to fetch them all a cup of hot chocolate.
Then she says; "Nettie, I am so glad you told us about your
adventure, and I'm very pleased you are safe, but now do
you understand why we don't want you to go on the Internet
on your own? We don't want you to be frightened."

"I know, and I'm sorry Grandma," says Nettie.

"And I'm sorry I took your tablet, Grandad. I was just so cross."

"Thank you," says Grandad. "Maybe, next time you're here,
we can play on the tablet together." So Grandpa takes his
tablet and puts it up on the shelf in his workshop.

And because Nettie was so brave and honest, he let
her keep her new friend Webby next to her bed.

Nettie snuggles up tight and dreams of the bunnies and flowers
and the fun parts of her adventure. She smiles to herself, dreaming
of all the great adventures she'll be able to have in Cyberland.

So, what do you think?

Why was Grandma cross with Nettie?

What happened when Nettie made Webby go into the forest?

Why is Nettie more frightened of the creatures
than she is of Grandma being cross?

Nettie, why were you allowed to keep little Webby next to your bed?

Because I was sorry, and I promised not to go on the Internet again without a guide nearby.

A Message for Parents, Family Members and Carers

One of the most important purposes of this book is to give you the chance to talk with the small child in your care about the Internet, the problems and concerns. You will need to talk to them about it someday, so starting now is a good time.

If you feel you would like more information about keeping young children safe online, there are a number of websites that can answer your questions and give you good advice.

These include:

Think U Know: guidance and resources for professionals, families and children. www.thinkuknow.co.uk

National Crime Agency's command for Child Exploitation and Online Protection www.ceop.police.uk/safety-centre

Information and advice on complaints procedures and reporting routes to social media providers about inappropriate content can be accessed at www.reportharmfulcontent.com

www.saferinternet.org.uk

www.stopitnow.org.uk/scotland

South West Grid for Learning: www.swgfl.org.uk/online-safety

www.nspcc.org.uk/keeping-children-safe/online-safety

www.getsafeonline.org and www.ncsc.gov.uk

www.young.scot/campaigns/national/digiaye

www.scotland.police.uk/youth-hub